A Dad's Gotta Do
What a Dad's Gotta Do

Story by
MARK JONES

Illustrated by
CHRISTA BREWER

Presented to

_____

_____

On

_____

Given by

_____

_____

One hundred percent of the net profits from the sale of this book will be donated to charity. The funds will be distributed primarily to organizations impacting children in need around the world.

For book orders/information: www.mrmarksclassroom.com

ISBN 978-0-9899416-0-0
© 2013 Mark Jones
© 2013 Christa Brewer, Illustrations

Author: Mark Jones
Illustrator: Christa Brewer
Book design and layout: BeGraphic/Jeffery Behymer

Manufactured in the U.S.A.

The illustrations were rendered in acrylic paint on paper.

www.mrmarksclassroom.com

Dedicated to Our Sons

Mark Jones Dedication:
Riding in that truck each morning with my two sons, Zachary and Wesley, might have seemed like a daily routine, but looking back now, it was a treasure.

You are a gift from God to me. I am very proud of you and deeply respect the men you have become. My love for you is indescribable.

Dad

Christa Brewer Dedication:
God searched the world over and picked you for us. You have brightened my life with your smile. I look forward to watching you discover the plan that God has for your life. Jacob, I love you always.

Mom

It was an ordinary Monday morning in an ordinary town for an ordinary dad and his two sons, Zac and Wes.

When it was time to go to school, they got into Dad's yellow truck and buckled their seatbelts. Dad and Zac smiled as they sang loudly with the radio, but Wes was too sleepy to join them.

As they joined the line of colorful vehicles circling the playground on their way to the drop-off entrance of Wes's school, the singing continued without missing a beat.

Except for one thing: Wes still had not made a peep.

"You haven't sung one word with us, Wes. Are you awake?" asked Dad. Wes just shrugged his shoulders, yawned, and continued to look out the window.

6

As Dad inched the yellow truck up the line little by little, he and Zac continued singing with great expression and at a great volume.

Dad and Zac never missed a word, yet Wes remained silent.

The music continued, but Dad stopped singing. Turning to Wes he said, "I love you, Wes. I hope you have a happy day." But Wes didn't answer.

Zac couldn't believe the way his brother was behaving. He wondered what Dad would do next.

Zac smiled as he watched Dad touch Wes's shoulder and say again, "I love you. I hope you have a happy day." But Wes didn't even move.

That's when Dad turned off the radio and said with his strong daddy voice, "Wes, did you hear me? I said I love you!"

10

Wes unbuckled his seatbelt and slipped into his backpack. But before Dad pulled up to the drop-off entrance, Wes opened the door and got out—without saying a word!

Dad was shocked! But then he did something no one could believe. Not even his sons.

12

Dad quickly rolled down the window and shouted so loud that everyone in the second grade heard him say, "I LOVE YOU, WES!"

Wes was now wide-awake, and he couldn't believe what his dad had just done in front of everyone. He began to run toward the school as Dad continued to shout, **"I LOVE YOU!"**

Wes was running at full speed as Dad pulled the yellow truck under the cover and began honking the horn.

When Wes ducked inside the school, he could still hear Dad shouting, "I LOVE YOU! **I LOVE YOU!**"

The teachers smiled, the students were shocked, and the parents were delighted as the dad showed his great love for his son.

W es couldn't believe his dad had just gone bonkers. But when he looked out the window, he smiled from ear to ear and chuckled so loud that others could hear.

As Dad waved good-bye to Wes, he heard Zac say from the back seat, "Dad…please don't do that to me!"

When they arrived at Zac's school, Dad thought, "A dad's gotta do what a dad's gotta do!"

So he turned to Zac, and with a smile said, "I love you, Zac. I hope you…"

But sooner than Dad could finish, Zac quickly said, "I love you, too, Dad!"—before anything could get out of hand.

The End

(But the dad's love never ended!)